IMAGINE THAT

Licensed exclusively to Imagine That Publishing Ltd
Tide Mill Way, Woodbridge, Suffolk, IP12 1AP, UK
www.imaginethat.com
Copyright © 2019 Imagine That Group Ltd
All rights reserved
0 2 4 6 8 9 7 5 3 1
Manufactured in China

Retold by Sarah Lucy
Illustrated by Kimberley Barnes

ISBN 978-1-78958-195-9

A catalogue record for this book is available from the British Library

G. B. de Villeneuve

Beauty and the Beast

Retold by Sarah Lucy
Illustrated by Kimberley Barnes

Once upon a time, there lived a rich merchant who had three daughters.

The youngest, Bella, had a particularly kind and loving heart and was soon called 'Beauty' by all who knew her.

Beauty's sisters enjoyed a life of sparkly necklaces, pretty dresses and fancy parties, but that was about to change.

One day, disaster struck and their father lost all of his money.

The older sisters shrieked and wept, but Beauty promised to work hard to help her family.

Although this pleased Beauty's father, he was determined to find their fortune once again.

'Don't come back without presents for us!' cried the two eldest sisters.

The merchant turned lovingly to Beauty, who had kept very quiet.

'And what would you like, Beauty?' he asked.

'All I wish for is a single red rose,' she replied, waving her father goodbye.

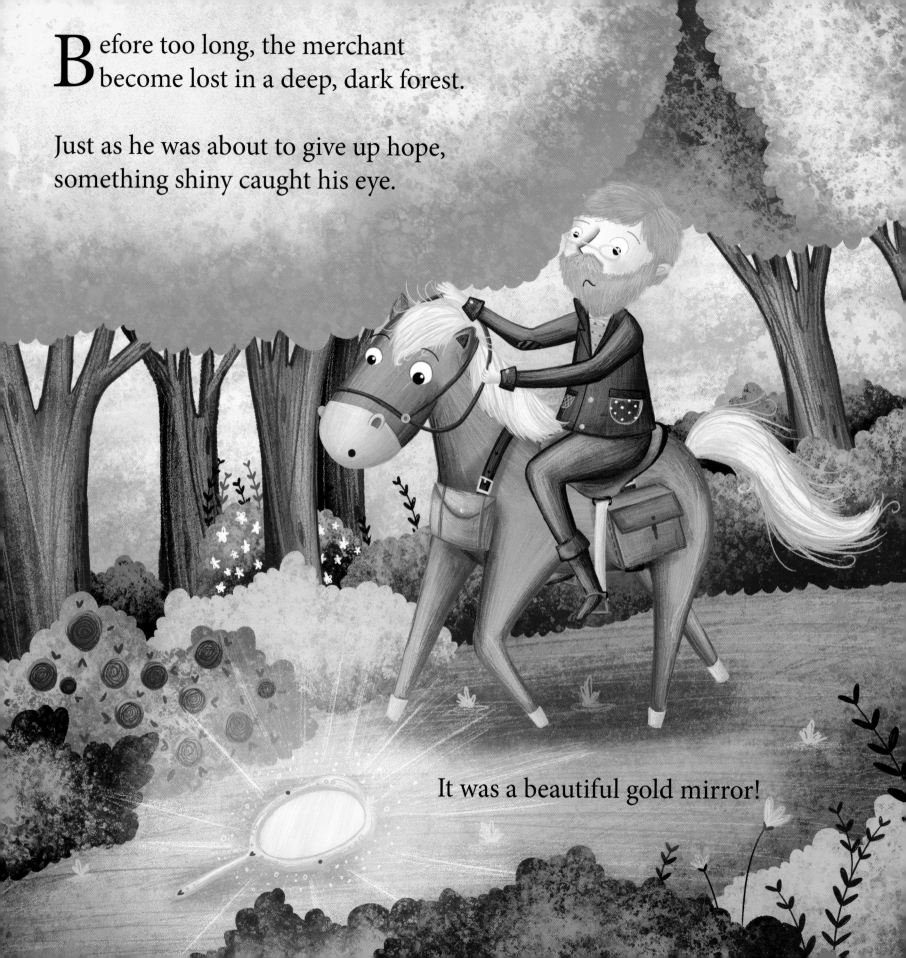

Before too long, the merchant become lost in a deep, dark forest.

Just as he was about to give up hope, something shiny caught his eye.

It was a beautiful gold mirror!

As the merchant picked up the mirror, he saw a big castle with swirls of mist surrounding it.

It was a magic mirror!

Suddenly, he was no longer in the deep, dark forest, but inside the castle!

The merchant looked around in amazement. 'Is anyone home?' he called, with a shake in his voice. No one replied.

The next morning, the merchant was surprised to find a delicious breakfast waiting for him.

After eating, the merchant decided to explore the castle gardens. As he looked at the beautiful roses, he remembered Beauty's request.

The merchant picked the most beautiful red rose he could find.

Suddenly, a shadow fell over him. He was face-to-face with the most hideous creature he had ever seen!

'How dare you steal a rose from me!' growled the Beast.

'Please don't hurt me!' said the merchant. 'It's for my daughter, Beauty.'

'Hmmm,' growled the Beast. 'Send me Beauty. Then I will make you rich again and set you free.'

Before the merchant had a chance to disagree with the Beast, he was sent back through the forest to his house. As he greeted his daughters, he told them the terrible news.

'Don't worry, father. You must not break your promise. I will go to the Beast,' Beauty said bravely.

When Beauty arrived at the Beast's castle, it was just as her father had described.

For days, Beauty ate alone and wandered around the castle, growing more and more lonely.

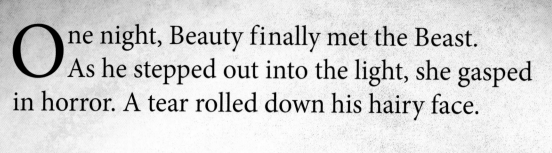

One night, Beauty finally met the Beast.
As he stepped out into the light, she gasped in horror. A tear rolled down his hairy face.

'I must be the ugliest thing you have ever seen,' he said sadly.

Beauty did not care how the Beast looked and soon they became friends.

The Beast gave Beauty the magic mirror, so she could see the outside world whenever she wanted.

Although Beauty loved spending time with her new friend, she missed her father. One night at dinner, she asked the Beast if she could visit her family.

The Beast agreed, but only if she took her magic mirror
with her so that she would not forget him.

Once home, Beauty greeted her father with joy.

'I'm so happy to have you back, Beauty,' her father cried.

For days, Beauty swept and baked and happily listened to her sisters chattering. The mirror stayed tucked under her pillow, forgotten about.

One night, Beauty suddenly remembered the magic mirror. Feeling bad, she peered into it and saw something terrible.

The beautiful roses in the Beast's garden were dying, and lying amongst them was the Beast, barely alive!

'I must go to him!' cried Beauty.

When Beauty finally reached the Beast, she wept, saying, 'Please don't die, Beast. I love you.'

Suddenly, the Beast's eyes opened and something amazing happened. Little by little, he began to change before Beauty's very eyes!

The Beast transformed into a handsome young prince!

'Who are you?' Beauty asked in amazement,
'Where is the Beast that I love?'

'I am the Beast,' replied the prince.
'Long ago, a witch cast a terrible spell
on me and turned me into an ugly beast.
To break the spell, someone had to love
me for myself, not for my looks.
Just like you have, Beauty.'

With the spell broken, the dying rose garden burst into life, spreading colour and sunshine over the entire castle.

As the thorns disappeared and the chirping of birds filled the air, Beauty and her prince knew that they would live happily ever after.